TIP-OFF
BASKETBALL

POWER
FORWARD

By Jason Glaser

Must
Read!

Gareth Stevens
Publishing

Please visit our Web site, www.garethstevens.com. For a free color catalog of all our high-quality books, call toll free 1-800-542-2595 or fax 1-877-542-2596.

Library of Congress Cataloging-in-Publication Data

Glaser, Jason.
Power forward / Jason Glaser.
   p. cm. — (Tip-off : basketball)
Includes index.
ISBN 978-1-4339-3978-5 (pbk.)
ISBN 978-1-4339-3979-2 (6 pack)
ISBN 978-1-4339-3977-8 (library binding)
1. Forwards (Basketball)—Juvenile literature. 2. Basketball—Offense—Juvenile literature. I. Title.
GV889.G56 2010
796.323—dc22

2010016537

First Edition

Published in 2011 by
Gareth Stevens Publishing
111 East 14th Street, Suite 349
New York, NY 10003

Copyright © 2011 Gareth Stevens Publishing

Designer: Haley W. Harasymiw
Editor: Greg Roza

Gareth Stevens Publishing would like to thank consultant Stephen Hayn, men's basketball coach at Dowling College, for his guidance in writing this book.

Photo credits: Cover, pp. 1, 30 Nick Laham/Getty Images; cover, back cover, pp. 2–3, 7, 17, 33, 39, 44–48 (background on all), pp. 12, 18, 19, 20, 23, 24, 25, 35, 41, 42 (basketball border on all), pp. 39, 42–43 Shutterstock.com; pp. 4, 5, 35, 45 Jed Jacobsohn/Getty Images; p. 6 George Eastman House/Getty Images; p. 7 Gjon Mili/Time Life Pictures/Getty Images; p. 8 Myron Davis/Time Life Pictures/Getty Images; pp. 9, 10, 11 Dick Raphael/NBAE via Getty Images; p. 12 (top) Focus on Sport/Getty Images; pp. 12 (bottom), 26 Andrew D. Bernstein/NBAE via Getty Images; p. 13 Stephen Dunn/Getty Images; p. 14 Dan Levine/AFP/Getty Images; pp. 15, 34 Lisa Blumenfeld/Getty Images; pp. 17, 33 Elsa/Getty Images; p. 18 Harry How/Getty Images; p. 19 Chris Graythen/Getty Images; pp. 20, 29 Noah Graham/NBAE via Getty Images; p. 21 Fernando Medina/NBAE via Getty Images; pp. 22, 25 Sam Forencich/NBAE via Getty Images; p. 23 Jonathan Newton/The Washington Post via Getty Images; p. 24 Scott Cunningham/NBAE via Getty Images; p. 27 Ron Turenne/NBAE via Getty Images; p. 28 Dale Tait/NBAE via Getty Images; p. 31 Clarke Evans/NBAE via Getty Images; p. 32 Ronald Martinez/Getty Images; p. 36 Kevin C. Cox/Getty Images; p. 37 Christian Peterson/Getty Images; pp. 38, 41 iStockphoto.com; p. 40 Melissa Majchrzak/NBAE/Getty Images; p. 44 Mike Powell/Getty Images.

Printed in the United States of America

CPSIA compliance information: Batch #CS10GS: For further information contact Gareth Stevens, New York, New York at 1-800-542-2595.

CONTENTS

Boldface words appear in the glossary.

With Great Power

Power forwards are big men who use great physical strength to make baskets, block shots, and position themselves for **rebounds**. Being a power forward takes a big player who can handle big responsibilities.

Leading by Example

On June 15, 2003, the San Antonio Spurs and the New Jersey Nets met in Game Six of the **NBA** Finals. The Nets led from the beginning. The Spurs' power forward, Tim Duncan, knew he had to motivate his team. Duncan scored over and over to tie the game just before **halftime**.

Tim Duncan makes a shot over three New Jersey Nets players.

4

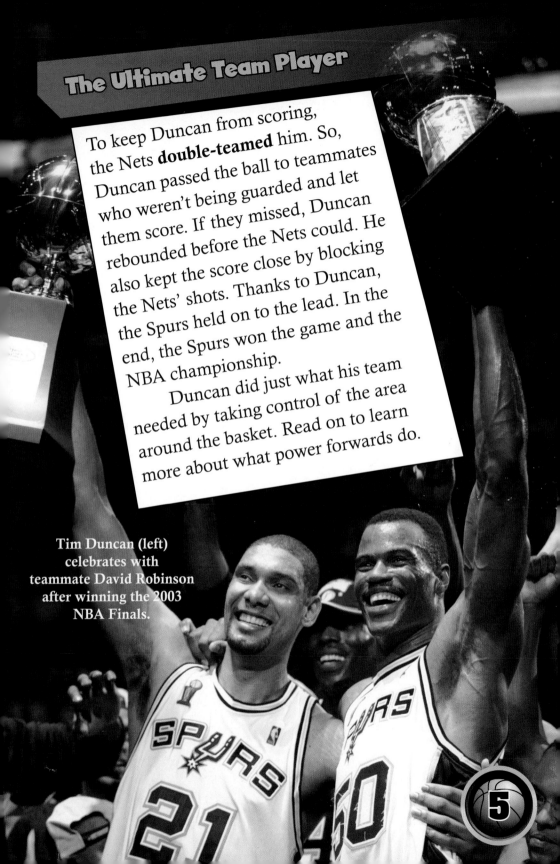

To keep Duncan from scoring, the Nets **double-teamed** him. So, Duncan passed the ball to teammates who weren't being guarded and let them score. If they missed, Duncan rebounded before the Nets could. He also kept the score close by blocking the Nets' shots. Thanks to Duncan, the Spurs held on to the lead. In the end, the Spurs won the game and the NBA championship.

Duncan did just what his team needed by taking control of the area around the basket. Read on to learn more about what power forwards do.

Tim Duncan (left) celebrates with teammate David Robinson after winning the 2003 NBA Finals.

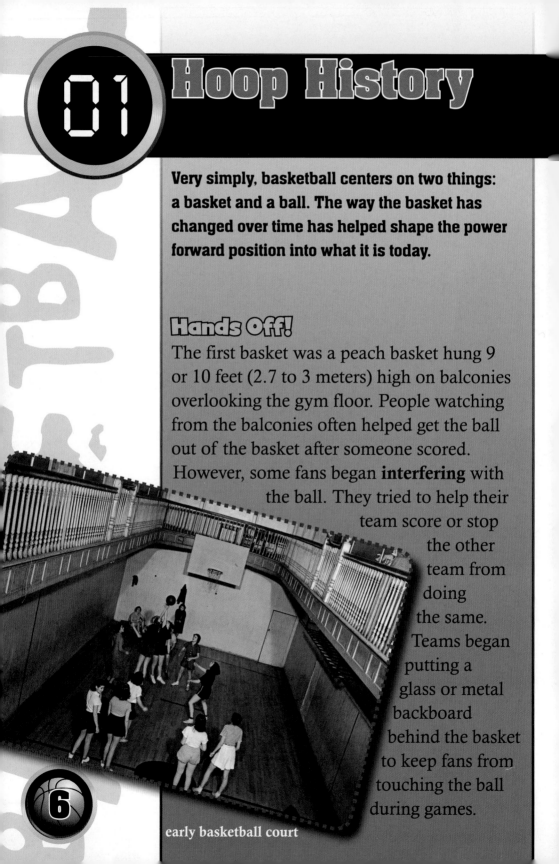

Hoop History

Very simply, basketball centers on two things: a basket and a ball. The way the basket has changed over time has helped shape the power forward position into what it is today.

Hands Off!

The first basket was a peach basket hung 9 or 10 feet (2.7 to 3 meters) high on balconies overlooking the gym floor. People watching from the balconies often helped get the ball out of the basket after someone scored. However, some fans began **interfering** with the ball. They tried to help their team score or stop the other team from doing the same. Teams began putting a glass or metal backboard behind the basket to keep fans from touching the ball during games.

early basketball court

With a backboard in place, missed shots bounced off the backboard and in front of the basket. Tall players quickly learned to bang a ball off the backboard and into the basket. Forwards learned how the backboard affected the ball and used that knowledge to score and rebound.

A power foward in 1944 uses the backboard to make a basket.

Even with the backboard, a close shot could still miss or get blocked. To put the ball into the basket, players began "climbing" the wall the basket hung from. Taking a step or two up the wall let them get high enough to stuff the ball into the basket without letting go. To keep players from doing this, a rule was added that baskets needed to be hung 2 feet (0.6 m) away from the wall. Even so, good jumpers could still **slam dunk** the ball into the basket without actually shooting it.

Bob Kurland, shown here in a photo from 1945, was one of the first players to slam dunk regularly during games.

8

Although he wasn't the first player to dunk, many fans consider Wilt Chamberlin to be basketball's first great dunker. He helped popularize the move in the 1960s.

High-Flying Offense

For a long time, many players and fans thought dunking the ball was unsportsmanlike. Dunking was against the rules in college and not done much in the NBA. In 1967, a second professional basketball league called the **ABA** formed. To make the games more exciting, they encouraged **offenses** to score using dunks. Seeing how much the fans liked it, NBA players also began dunking. By 1976, dunking was made legal in college as well.

Looking Back at Forwards

The role of the power forward has changed through the efforts of the position's greatest stars. Let's take a look at historic power forwards who've helped shape the modern game.

The Father of the Power Forward

Many basketball experts consider Bob Pettit to be the first power forward ever. When Pettit entered the NBA in 1954, players thought only about scoring. Pettit focused on all the missed shots. By controlling the area around and under the basket, he became a great rebounder. He got over 1,000 rebounds in nine of his 11 seasons. By turning offensive rebounds into follow-up shots, Pettit became the first NBA player to reach 20,000 points in a career.

Basketball great Bill Russell once said, "Bob made 'second effort' a part of the sport's vocabulary."

DeBusschere makes a shot against the Boston Celtics during the 1973 Eastern Conference Finals.

To keep Dave DeBusschere from leaving the Detroit Pistons to play professional baseball, the team made an unusual decision. They let their star player be their coach as well. DeBusschere was a smart player and outstanding on **defense**. He guided his team in shutting down other teams' offenses and contributed an average of 11 rebounds per game. When he was traded to the New York Knicks in 1969, he was free to concentrate on playing his best basketball. He helped the Knicks win championships in 1970 and 1973.

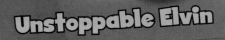

Elvin Hayes

A combination of endurance, patience, and an accurate turnaround **jump shot** made Elvin Hayes one of the highest scorers in NBA history. From 1968 to 1984, Hayes made more than 16,000 rebounds and scored 27,000 points. A tireless player, he also led the league in minutes played four times.

McAdoo Can Do

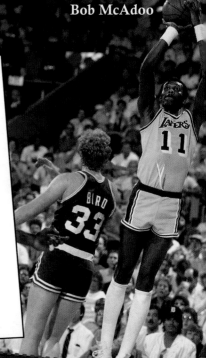

Bob McAdoo

When Bob McAdoo entered the NBA in 1972, he was a scoring machine. He led the league in scoring 3 years in a row, starting with the 1973–1974 season. He was a rare power forward who was also a good outside shooter. Injuries troubled him for many years, but he still won two championships with the Los Angeles Lakers in 1982 and 1985.

Kevin McHale of the Boston Celtics used to call the area around him on the court "the torture chamber." No one could guard McHale near the basket. With his long arms, accurate shot, and excellent footwork, McHale's dominance close to the basket helped the Celtics win championships in 1981, 1984, and 1986.

McHale makes a shot against the Golden State Warriors in 1988.

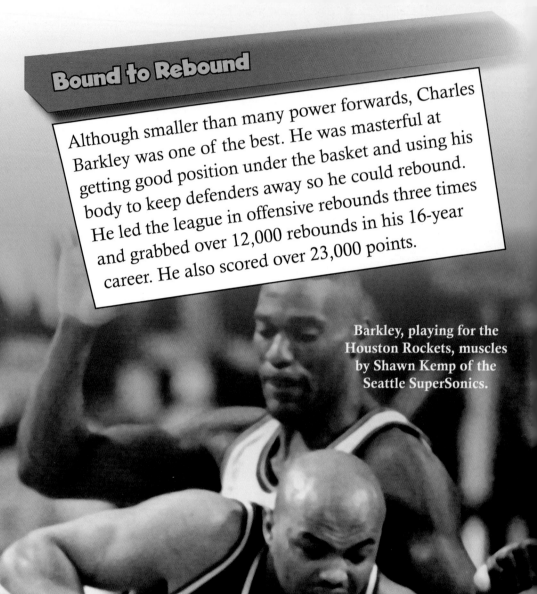

Bound to Rebound

Although smaller than many power forwards, Charles Barkley was one of the best. He was masterful at getting good position under the basket and using his body to keep defenders away so he could rebound. He led the league in offensive rebounds three times and grabbed over 12,000 rebounds in his 16-year career. He also scored over 23,000 points.

Barkley, playing for the Houston Rockets, muscles by Shawn Kemp of the Seattle SuperSonics.

Karl Malone's physical style near the net was effective but **controversial**. Malone knew just how to bump other players to make it look as if they had **fouled** him. He led the league in **free-throw** attempts seven times and free-throw points eight times. Malone's aggressiveness also made him a great rebounder. He has more free throws and more defensive rebounds than anyone in NBA history. In 18 seasons with the Utah Jazz and one with the Los Angeles Lakers, Malone also shot for almost 37,000 points.

Malone earned the nickname "the Mailman" in college because he was a very dependable player. Malone "always delivered" when his team needed him.

03 Playing with Power

Scoring points usually isn't the first thing on a power forward's mind. Most plays are designed to get the ball to the shooting guard, small forward, or center. The power forward's job is to grab rebounds and help his teammates score. Being a power forward means getting ready to mix it up with other players near the basket and fighting for every ball that comes off the rim. Here's what being a power forward is all about.

Controlling the Post

Power forwards spend most of their time in an area called the post. This is the area between the free-throw line and the baseline. Power forwards "post up" by keeping their back to the basket. When they receive a pass, they turn and make a shot around or over a defender. The area right beneath the basket is the "low post," and the area closer to the free-throw line is the "high post."

shooting guard 2

point guard 1

free-throw line

power forward 4

POST

center 5

small forward 3

baseline

Kevin Garnett, power forward for the Boston Celtics, takes a shot in a game against the Denver Nuggets.

The power forward isn't the only player who must worry about the post. The team's biggest man, the center, will drive in near the basket to score or help with rebounds. The small forward usually plays against the other team's smaller defenders on the side of the basket opposite the power forward. These two players draw defenders away from the basket to let the power forward rebound and score up close.

On offense, a power forward's first responsibility is to help teammates score. One way to do this is through a pick. The power forward uses his large body as an obstacle to keep **opponents** away from the shooter. Picking defenders near the basket can open up a close, easy shot for a teammate. A power forward can also run this play to help a teammate without the ball get open for a pass. This version of the play is called a screen.

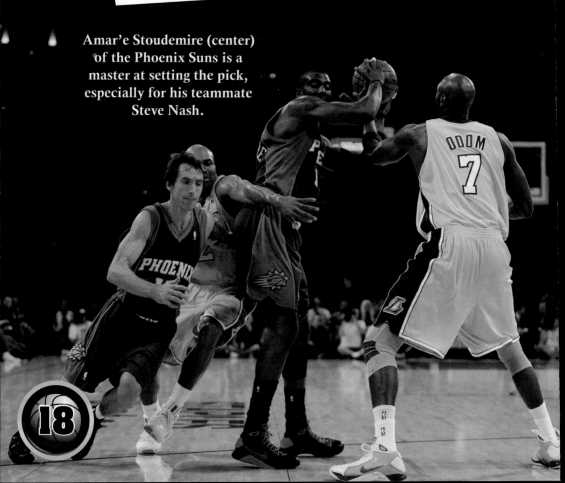

Amar'e Stoudemire (center) of the Phoenix Suns is a master at setting the pick, especially for his teammate Steve Nash.

If a play goes well, the power forward isn't likely to score, but he should always be ready! By standing near the basket, an open forward will have a chance to put the ball in from up close. A power forward can choose from several short-range shots. He can put a quick jump shot in the net, **layup** off the backboard, or roll it in off his hand from the baseline. He can also shoot from his outside hand and make a **hook shot** over a defender!

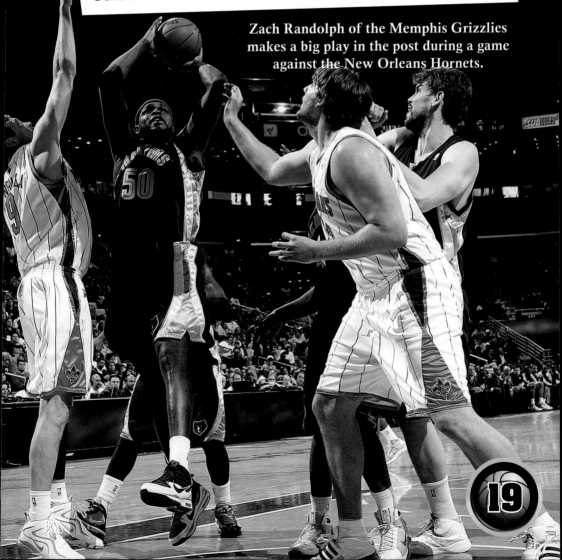

Zach Randolph of the Memphis Grizzlies makes a big play in the post during a game against the New Orleans Hornets.

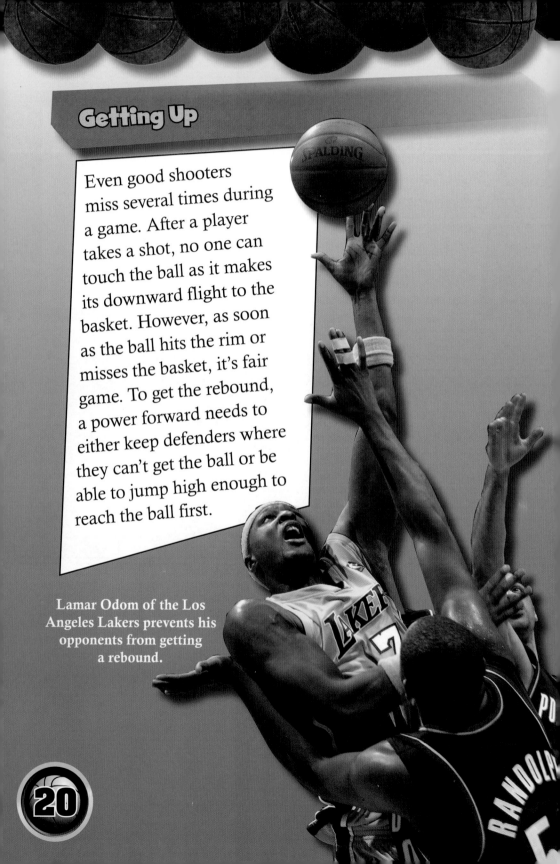

Getting Up

Even good shooters miss several times during a game. After a player takes a shot, no one can touch the ball as it makes its downward flight to the basket. However, as soon as the ball hits the rim or misses the basket, it's fair game. To get the rebound, a power forward needs to either keep defenders where they can't get the ball or be able to jump high enough to reach the ball first.

Lamar Odom of the Los Angeles Lakers prevents his opponents from getting a rebound.

Once the power forward catches a rebound, the other team's players will swarm him and try to get the ball back. The forward may take a shot. Most of the time, however, the rush of defenders leaves a teammate open. Good power forwards spot open teammates and quickly get the ball to one of them.

During a game against the Milwaukee Bucks, Rashard Lewis of the Orlando Magic prepares to grab a rebound.

Strong on the Weak Side

Many times, a power forward positions himself on the "weak" side of the basket—the side with fewer players. By standing across from so many possible shooters, the power forward has the best chance of rebounding a missed shot.

On Defense

As we've seen, the power forward is a vital part of the offensive game. However, the power forward plays an equally important role on defense.

Always Ready

Controlling the area around the basket is even trickier on defense. Power forwards need to know who's moving toward the basket while keeping track of the ball. They need to know where to go for a rebound. A power forward guards the baseline to keep opponents from crossing underneath the basket. He may have to come away from the baseline to stop an incoming pass, but he can't let the player he's guarding get open behind him.

Carlos Boozer of the Utah Jazz guards LaMarcus Aldridge of the Portland Trail Blazers and keeps him from reaching the baseline.

Building Blocks

On defense, a power forward needs to be a good jumper and have perfect timing to block shots. If the opponent pulls up or jumps to shoot, the power forward can jump up at the same time. By jumping high enough at the right time, the forward can swat the ball away as it leaves the shooter's hands. He must be careful, though, not to get fooled by a fake shot, or he'll be in the air while his opponent **dribbles** by!

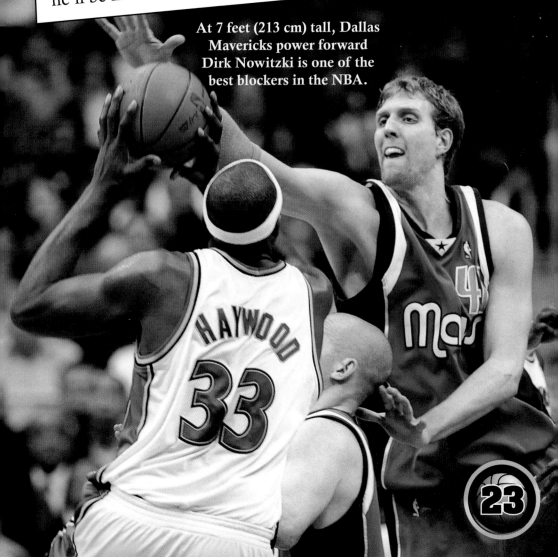

At 7 feet (213 cm) tall, Dallas Mavericks power forward Dirk Nowitzki is one of the best blockers in the NBA.

Defensive Rebounding

A power forward on defense must be ready to get a missed shot just as he would on offense. Once a shot is taken, the power forward must get in position and try to outjump the other team's players. Getting a defensive rebound is the easiest way to shut down the other team's chance to score.

The Atlanta Hawks' Josh Smith grabs a defensive rebound during a game against the Detroit Pistons.

Even when the power forward gets the ball on defense and passes it to a teammate, his work is just beginning! He must now run all the way from the opponent's basket into position near his own. The power forward probably has to run farther—and faster—on a **turnover** than any other player. He must be in position by the time his team makes it across the court to increase his chances of getting the offensive rebound on a missed shot.

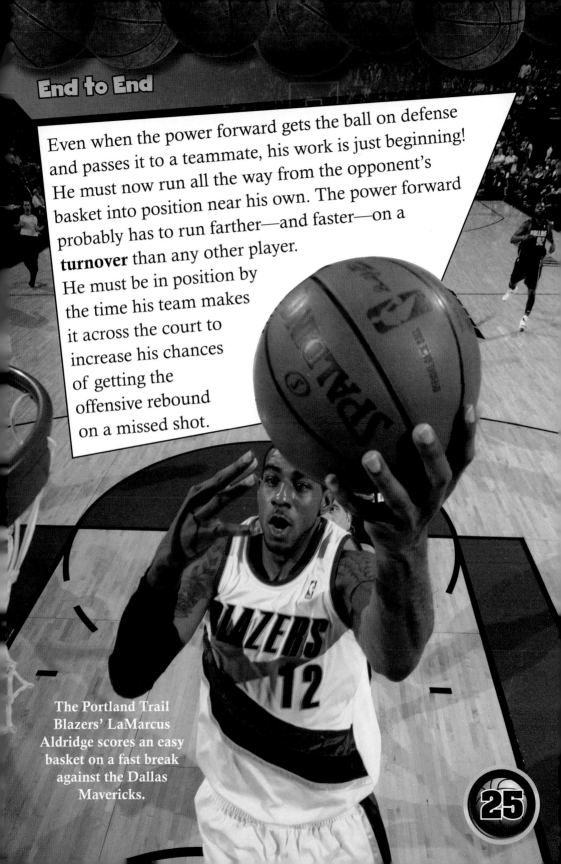

The Portland Trail Blazers' LaMarcus Aldridge scores an easy basket on a fast break against the Dallas Mavericks.

Key Skills

Power forward is a very physical, demanding position. If a player can't measure up, his team is sure to lose plenty of rebounds—and games!

Getting Your Rear in Gear

As silly as it may sound, one of a power forward's most important tools is his butt! Power forwards stand in a low crouch with feet wide and arms spread apart for good balance. This stance gives the power forward an advantage. By pushing their bottoms out behind them against opposing players, forwards can force their opponents back in a way that doesn't cause a foul. This move is called "**boxing out**."

David West of the New Orleans Hornets boxes out his opponent while going for a rebound without committing a foul.

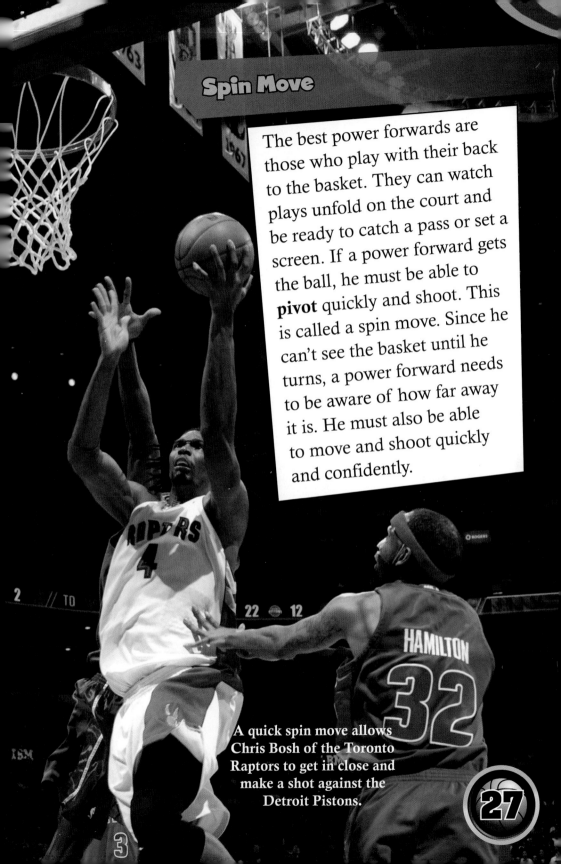

The best power forwards are those who play with their back to the basket. They can watch plays unfold on the court and be ready to catch a pass or set a screen. If a power forward gets the ball, he must be able to **pivot** quickly and shoot. This is called a spin move. Since he can't see the basket until he turns, a power forward needs to be aware of how far away it is. He must also be able to move and shoot quickly and confidently.

A quick spin move allows Chris Bosh of the Toronto Raptors to get in close and make a shot against the Detroit Pistons.

27

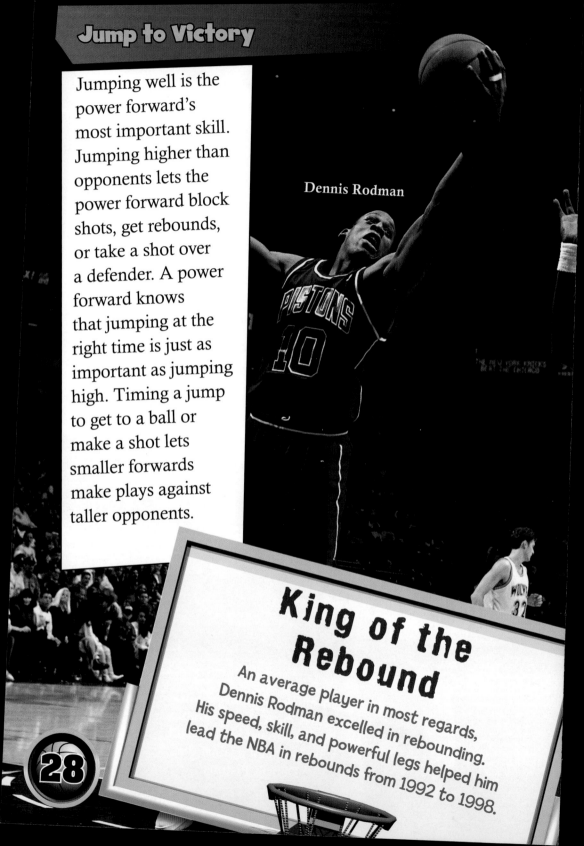

Jumping well is the power forward's most important skill. Jumping higher than opponents lets the power forward block shots, get rebounds, or take a shot over a defender. A power forward knows that jumping at the right time is just as important as jumping high. Timing a jump to get to a ball or make a shot lets smaller forwards make plays against taller opponents.

Dennis Rodman

King of the Rebound

An average player in most regards, Dennis Rodman excelled in rebounding. His speed, skill, and powerful legs helped him lead the NBA in rebounds from 1992 to 1998.

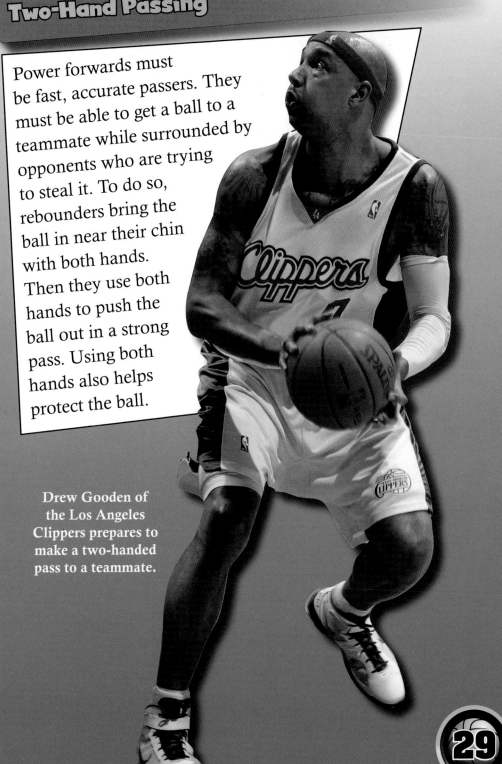

Power forwards must be fast, accurate passers. They must be able to get a ball to a teammate while surrounded by opponents who are trying to steal it. To do so, rebounders bring the ball in near their chin with both hands. Then they use both hands to push the ball out in a strong pass. Using both hands also helps protect the ball.

Drew Gooden of the Los Angeles Clippers prepares to make a two-handed pass to a teammate.

Ready to Play

Power forwards have to be ready both mentally and physically in order to play their best on the court.

Know Your Team

For power forwards, studying the playbook isn't just about setting up shots. Knowing where the shot will come from lets the forward set good screens and get in position for a rebound. Lots of team practice lets forwards see how their teammates shoot and where the ball is likely to go.

Al Harrington of the New York Knicks dunks the ball against the Utah Jazz during a game in the Knicks' home court—Madison Square Garden.

Follow the Bouncing Ball

Power forwards should study how balls bounce off their home court's rims. The better a power forward knows how far out missed shots will go, the better the home-court advantage will be.

Pau Gasol of the Los Angeles Lakers uses his strength and endurance to muscle past a defender during a game against the San Antonio Spurs.

Hit the Gym

Athletes need to be in great shape. Power forwards especially need to work their arms and legs. They'll be jumping and bumping all game long. Having strong limbs and balance will help them keep the ball out of their opponents' hands.

Today's Superstars

Here are a few of the players in the NBA who've made names for themselves as power forwards.

The Big Fundamental

The San Antonio Spurs have one of the greatest all-around players ever in Tim Duncan. Night after night, Duncan blocks, steals, rebounds, scores from up close, and scores from far away. He's so good at everything that teammates call him "the Big **Fundamental**." Duncan's helped make the Spurs one of the most successful teams in professional sports. He's won four championships with them and been named Finals **MVP** three times. He's one of only four people with that honor. Duncan has also been league MVP twice.

Duncan takes a shot against the Phoenix Suns during the 2010 NBA playoffs.

The Big Ticket

Kevin Garnett won league MVP in 2004 because people had come to realize what Minnesota fans had known for years: the Timberwolves couldn't win without him. For years, Garnett made opposing teams regret missed shots. He led the league in defensive rebounds for 5 years and pulled down over 1,000 rebounds for three straight seasons. After being traded in 2007, Garnett helped the Boston Celtics win a championship as well.

Garnett is sometimes called "the Big Ticket" because he helped draw sell-out crowds to the Minnesota Timberwolves' home arena—the Target Center.

33

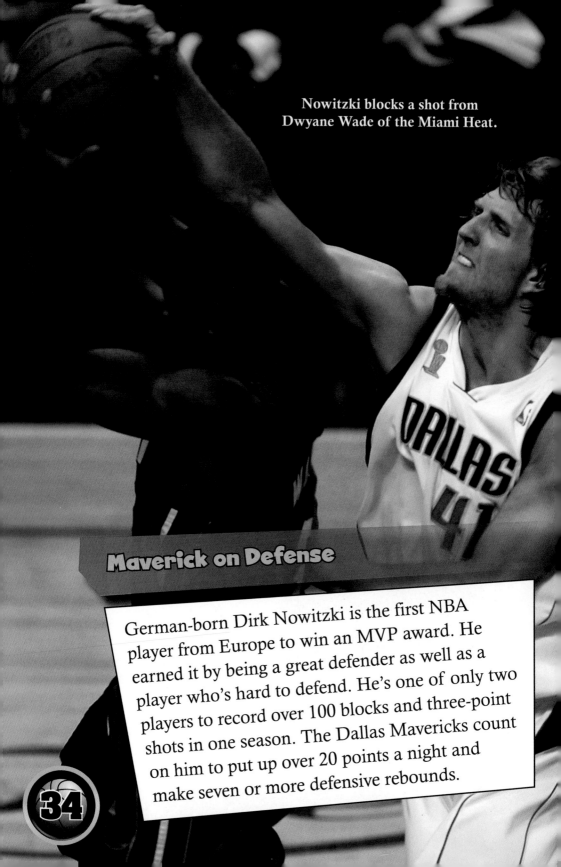

Nowitzki blocks a shot from
Dwyane Wade of the Miami Heat.

Maverick on Defense

German-born Dirk Nowitzki is the first NBA player from Europe to win an MVP award. He earned it by being a great defender as well as a player who's hard to defend. He's one of only two players to record over 100 blocks and three-point shots in one season. The Dallas Mavericks count on him to put up over 20 points a night and make seven or more defensive rebounds.

"Pau"-er Forward

Many people thought of Pau Gasol as a big fish in a small pond. He was the best player on the Memphis Grizzlies, but the Grizzlies were barely a playoff team. He was a great passer, accurate shooter, and steady rebounder, but didn't have a championship. Two years after being traded to the Los Angeles Lakers, Gasol played some of his finest basketball and helped the team to a championship in 2009.

Gasol won the 2001 NBA Rookie of the Year award when he was with the Grizzlies.

In the short history of the Toronto Raptors, Chris Bosh is probably the team's most popular player. This exciting power forward lights up the boards as both a scorer and a rebounder. He's averaged over 20 points a game and nearly 10 rebounds a game since 2006. Bosh is also one of the team's best shooters. When he misses, he's so quick he sometimes gets his own rebound.

Bosh's nickname, CB4, comes from his initials and his jersey number.

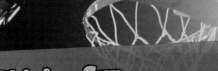
Shining Sun

Amar'e Stoudemire of the Phoenix Suns is different from most power forwards. He's not known for his defensive abilities. Stoudemire makes his mark on the game by catching passes or grabbing rebounds in the post and turning them into points. Despite his large size, Stoudemire springs into action in a flash, driving to the basket through defenders for thunderous slam dunks.

Stoudemire makes a jump shot against the Portland Trail Blazers during the 2010 NBA playoffs.

05 Future Star: You!

Looking for ways to improve your game at power forward? Try working on the fundamental skills covered in this chapter.

Fast Passing

Power forwards must pass quickly and accurately to get the ball to a teammate before being surrounded after catching a pass or rebound. Stand in a triangle with two friends. Pass one ball around the triangle as quickly as possible. You can make it harder by adding a second ball. This drill will train you to react quickly when your teammate's ready for a pass.

Keep your elbows pointed out to protect the ball as you move.

When rebounding, positioning and body control are just as important as jumping. Getting the best position means you won't have to outjump an opponent for the ball. Practice with two friends. While one shoots, compete with the other for rebounds with no jumping allowed. Look for the best position for getting the ball. Use your body to box out your opponent. Use your arms to bring the ball down where only you can get a hand on it.

Jump, Jump, Jump!

Jumping rope strengthens your legs and gets you hopping many times quickly. This can help you jump higher and faster during a game.

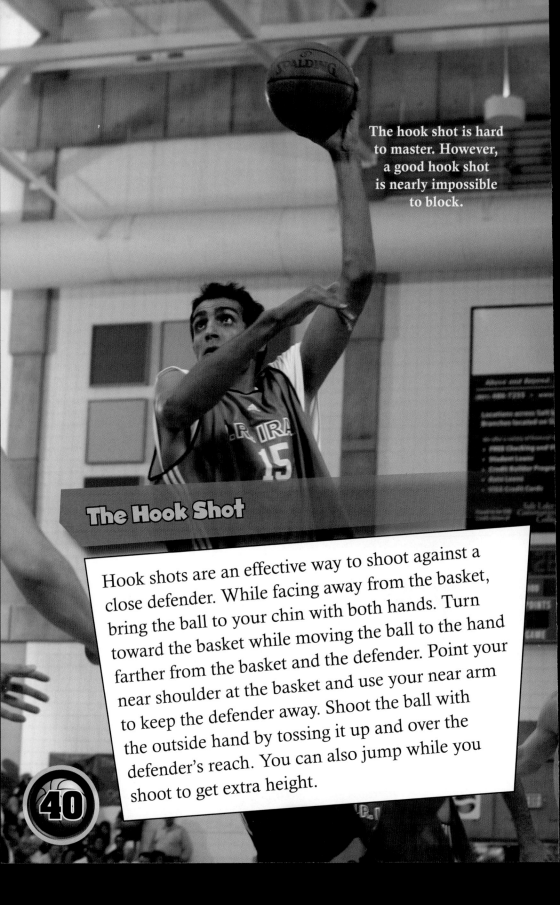

The hook shot is hard to master. However, a good hook shot is nearly impossible to block.

The Hook Shot

Hook shots are an effective way to shoot against a close defender. While facing away from the basket, bring the ball to your chin with both hands. Turn toward the basket while moving the ball to the hand farther from the basket and the defender. Point your near shoulder at the basket and use your near arm to keep the defender away. Shoot the ball with the outside hand by tossing it up and over the defender's reach. You can also jump while you shoot to get extra height.

Pass and Pivot

This exercise combines many important power forward skills—passing, positioning, pivoting, and shooting. Start on one side of the low post, facing the basket, with a friend standing in the opposite **wing**. Pass the ball and quickly cross the free-throw lane to catch a pass on the other side with your back to the basket. Pivot around on one foot and take a shot. Be sure to go after your own rebound! Make sure to practice pivoting on the other foot as well and starting from both sides of the low post.

It's important to protect the ball when pivoting to stop the opponent from stealing it.

41

Shoot, Pass, Move

For this drill, have a friend shoot toward the basket while you rebound. Have your friend yell "shoot," "pass," or "move." If he yells "shoot," take a shot or make a layup off the rebound. If he yells "pass," fake the shot but then pass back to your friend. If he yells "move," dribble quickly to the other side of the basket and layup. This will help both your skills and your reaction time on the court.

Although height helps, it's often more important in basketball to be quick on your feet.

Low dribbling keeps the ball under your control and away from your opponent's reach.

Ball Control

Taller players can lose the ball on steals by smaller players. Power forwards should work on a low dribble that gives them better control. With your legs spread apart to form a good base, crouch forward with your weight over your legs. Bounce the ball low to the ground 20 times with one hand. The ball should not come up higher than your knee. Handle the ball with the pads of your fingertips. Keep your head up and eyes forward, rather than watching the ball. Practice this with one hand, then the other, and finally bounce the ball back and forth between your hands.

Record Book

Who are the best power forwards in the history of the NBA? Let's check the record book to find out.

Career Blocks by a Power Forward:
1. Tim Duncan (still active)   **2,235** (as of 5/9/10)
2. George Johnson   **2,082**
3. Larry Nance   **2,027**
4. Kevin Garnett (still active)   **1,790** (as of 5/20/10)
5. Elvin Hayes   **1,771**

Blocks in a Season by a Power Forward:
1. George Johnson   **278**   1980–1981
2. George Johnson   **274**   1977–1978
3. George Johnson   **258**   1979–1980
4. Bob McAdoo   **246**   1973–1974
5. Larry Nance   **243**   1991–1992

Blocks in a Game by a Power Forward:
1. Larry Nance   **11**   01/07/1987
2. Andrei Kirilenko (still active)   **10**   03/25/2006
    Josh Smith (still active)   **10**   12/18/2004
    Amar'e Stoudemire (still active)   **10**   02/07/2004
    Shawn Kemp   **10**   01/18/1991
    Larry Nance   **10**   01/04/1988

Larry Nance

Rebounds in a Season by a Power Forward:

1. Jerry Lucas	**1,668**	1965–1966
2. Spencer Haywood	**1,637**	1969–1970
3. Jerry Lucas	**1,560**	1967–1968
4. Jerry Lucas	**1,547**	1966–1967
5. Bob Pettit	**1,540**	1960–1961

Career Rebounds by a Power Forward:

1. Elvin Hayes	**16,279**
2. Karl Malone	**14,968**
3. Wes Unseld	**13,769**
4. Buck Williams	**13,017**
5. Jerry Lucas	**12,942**

All-Star Game Appearances by a Power Forward:

1. Karl Malone	14
2. Kevin Garnett (still active)	13
3. Tim Duncan (still active)	12
Elvin Hayes	12
5. Charles Barkley	11
Elgin Baylor	11
Bob Pettit	11

Karl Malone

Glossary

ABA: American Basketball Association, a professional basketball league that existed from 1967 to 1976

box out: to use your body to force an opponent into a worse position

controversial: something that causes arguments

defense: the team trying to stop the other team from scoring

double-team: when two people defend against a single player

dribble: to move around the court while bouncing the ball

foul: a penalty called for breaking rules, usually coming from illegal contact between players

free throw: a chance to shoot for one point after being fouled; the shot is made from a line in front of the basket with no defenders

fundamental: a basic skill for a sport, such as shooting or passing

halftime: a break taken halfway through a game to give teams a chance to rest and make changes to their game plans

hook shot: a shot made over the head with the hand that is farther from the basket

interfere: to keep a game from being played properly

jump shot: a shot taken while jumping into the air

layup: a shot made from beneath the basket by bouncing the ball off the backboard and into the net

MVP: most valuable player

NBA: National Basketball Association, the men's professional basketball league in the United States; the NBA also includes the Toronto (Canada) Raptors

offense: the team trying to score

opponent: the person or team you must beat to win a game

pivot: to spin around on one foot that stays on the ground

rebound: a ball recovered off a missed shot

slam dunk: to throw the basketball into the basket from above the rim

turnover: when a team loses control of the ball to the opponent

wing: a spot where the free-throw line would cross over the three-point line if the free-throw line were extended

For More Information

Books

Doeden, Matt. *The World's Greatest Basketball Players.* Mankato, MN: Capstone Press, 2010.

Schaller, Bob, and Dave Harnish. *The Everything Kids' Basketball Book.* Avon, MA: Adams Media, 2009.

Slade, Suzanne. *Basketball: How It Works.* Mankato, MN: Capstone Press, 2010.

Web Sites

www.hoophall.com
Learn about the history of basketball at the online version of the Naismith Memorial Basketball Hall of Fame. Read the biographies of the greatest basketball players of all time.

www.nba.com
The official Web site of the National Basketball Association has information about teams and players both current and historic. Fans can see video, get news, check scores, and look over game or season statistics.

www.nba.com/kids
The NBA's official Web site for kids lets you play games, join fan clubs for your favorite team, and learn exercises to make you a better basketball player.

www.sikids.com/basketball/nba
The *Sports Illustrated* site for kids lets you follow your favorite NBA team. On this site, you'll find scores and news updates about your favorite sport.

Index

About the Author

Jason Glaser is a freelance writer and stay-at-home father living in Mankato, Minnesota. He has written over fifty nonfiction books for children including books on sports stars like Tim Duncan. When he isn't listening to sports radio or writing, Jason likes to play volleyball and put idealized versions of himself in sports video games.